the 12 mehs of Christmas

by gudetama™

PENGUIN WORKSHOP
An Imprint of Penguin Random House LLC, New York

Visit us online at www.penguinrandomhouse.com.

ISBN 9781524793586

10 9 8 7 6 5 4 3 2 1

the 12 mehs of Christmas

by gudetama™

text by Max Bisantz & Francesco Sedita

Penguin Workshop

On the first MEH of Christmas, my true love sent to me

a hot cup of matcha green tea.

meh...

On the second MEH of Christmas, my true love sent to me

two Swiss rolls
and a hot cup of matcha green tea.

I prefer soy sauce

On the third MEH
of Christmas, my true
love sent to me

three Russian dolls,
two Swiss rolls,
and a hot cup of matcha green tea.

nyet

On the fourth MEH
of Christmas, my true
love sent to me

four strips of bacon,
three Russian dolls,
two Swiss rolls,
and a hot cup of matcha green tea.

I'm sleepy

On the fifth MEH
of Christmas, my true
love sent to me

five jars of mayo,
four strips of bacon,
three Russian dolls,
two Swiss rolls,
and a hot cup of matcha green tea.

On the sixth MEH
of Christmas, my true
love sent to me

six chicks a-laying,
five jars of mayo,
four strips of bacon,
three Russian dolls,
two Swiss rolls,
and a hot cup of matcha green tea.

On the seventh MEH of Christmas, my true love sent to me

seven candles burning,
six chicks a-laying,
five jars of mayo,
four strips of bacon,
three Russian dolls,
two Swiss rolls,
and a hot cup of matcha green tea.

darkness is my friend

On the eighth MEH of Christmas, my true love sent to me

eight snakes a-slithering,
seven candles burning,
six chicks a-laying,
five jars of mayo,
four strips of bacon,
three Russian dolls,
two Swiss rolls,
and a hot cup of matcha green tea.

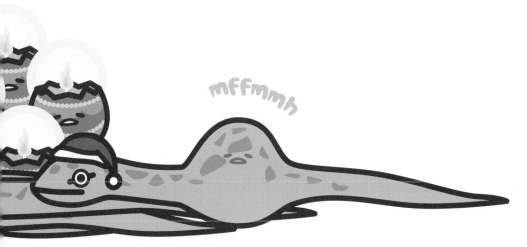
mffmmh

On the ninth MEH
of Christmas, my true
love sent to me

nine cameras snapping,
eight snakes a-slithering,
seven candles burning,
six chicks a-laying,
five jars of mayo,
four strips of bacon,
three Russian dolls,
two Swiss rolls,
and a hot cup of matcha green tea.

no pictures

On the tenth MEH of Christmas, my true love sent to me

ten deviled eggs a-leaping,
nine cameras snapping,
eight snakes a-slithering,
seven candles burning,
six chicks a-laying,
five jars of mayo,
four strips of bacon,
three Russian dolls,
two Swiss rolls,
and a hot cup of matcha green tea.

eleven pans a-sizzling,
ten deviled eggs a-leaping,
nine cameras snapping,
eight snakes a-slithering,
seven candles burning,
six chicks a-laying,
five jars of mayo,
four strips of bacon,
three Russian dolls,
two Swiss rolls,
and a hot cup of matcha green tea.

On the twelfth MEH of Christmas, my true love sent to me

twelve phones a-buzzing,
eleven pans a-sizzling,
ten deviled eggs a-leaping,
nine cameras snapping,
eight snakes a-slithering,
seven candles burning,
six chicks a-laying,
five jars of mayo,
four strips of bacon,
three Russian dolls,
two Swiss rolls,
and a hot cup of matcha green tea.

don't leave
a message

is Christmas over yet?